For
Freddie

An Imprint of Sterling Publishing
387 Park Avenue South
New York, NY 10016

This 2013 edition published by Sandy Creek.
First published in 2012 by Andersen Press under the title
My Friend Nigel.

ISBN 978-1-4351-4755-3

Manufactured in Johor, Malaysia.
Lot #:
2 4 6 8 10 9 7 5 3 1
02/13

MY
AMAZING
PET SNAIL

Sandy Creek
NEW YORK

JO HODGKINSON

Billy's dad and Billy's mom
Thought magic was a lot of fun.
You might think Bill would like it too
But quite the opposite was true.

KAZAM'S
MAGIC KIT
FOR
BEGINNERS

Billy's Mum & Dad
Flat 10
Fifth Floor
Appt: 1.

THE
MAGIC
OF
FLIGHT

Dad's flying tricks did not go well
Mom's potions made a nasty smell.

While they liked magic quite a lot . . .

Billy certainly did not.

Bill peered at all their
strange supplies
Jellied bugs and pickled flies.
Bubbling potions,
lizard's scales,

And what was this?
A little snail?

"Oh, Mom, please no!
Don't tell me he
Is for a magic recipe.

To do that would be so unkind
I have a better plan in mind.

Instead why don't you
say you'll let
Me keep this snail
as my new pet?"

Bill gave him Nigel
as a name,

He taught him how to play new games.

Said Dad to Mom, "Just give him time
He'll soon get bored of all that slime.

These spells will help us show our boy
Some other pets he could enjoy."

"We know you're
fond of your pet snail,

But have you thought about a **Whale?**

If not a whale, now let me see . . .
Perhaps a giant dancing bee!

This elephant does tricks you know
Unlike your snail who's rather slow.

This tiger here could be your guy
While Nigel is a little shy."

"I'm sorry but they'll have to go!
Oh, Mom and Dad, why can't you see?
It's Nigel who's the pet for me."

But what Bill said,
he said too late
And Nigel didn't
hear his mate.

As Billy turned
to see his snail,
He saw instead
a slimy trail.

It read:

I think it's for the best,
I'm not as fun as all the rest.
I hope you find the perfect pet
And I'm so happy that we met.
I'm sorry that it had to end.
Lots of love from,
your old friend
XXX

As Billy shouted Nigel's name,
Dad's magic spells
went wrong again.
Things got crazy,
things went bad.

The tiger tried to eat Bill's dad.
While Mom was being tickled silly,

The bee flew up and stung poor Billy.

As Nigel reached
the elevator,
He heard Bill's cry
and, as a skater,

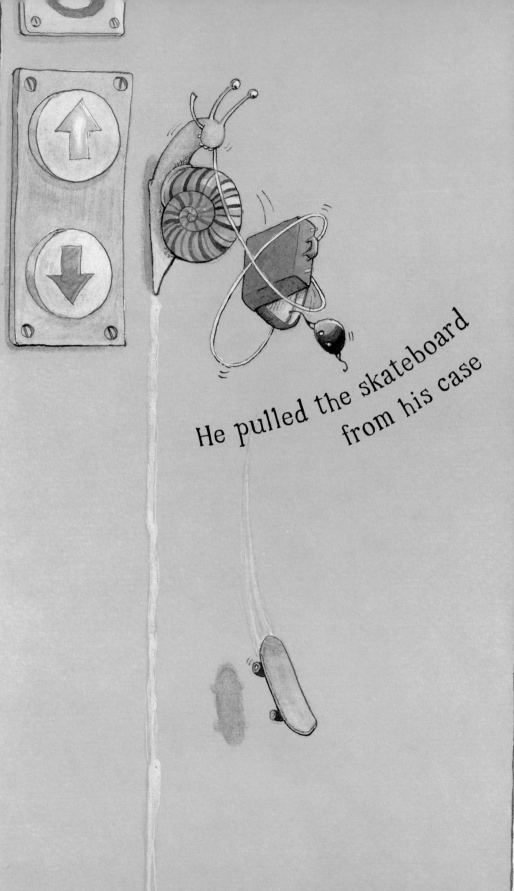

He pulled the skateboard
from his case

And WHIZZED along at lightning pace.

Then catapulted through the door,
And slid across the hallway floor.

But no one noticed Nigel Snail,
Or saw his super-slimy trail.

The tiger slipped onto his back

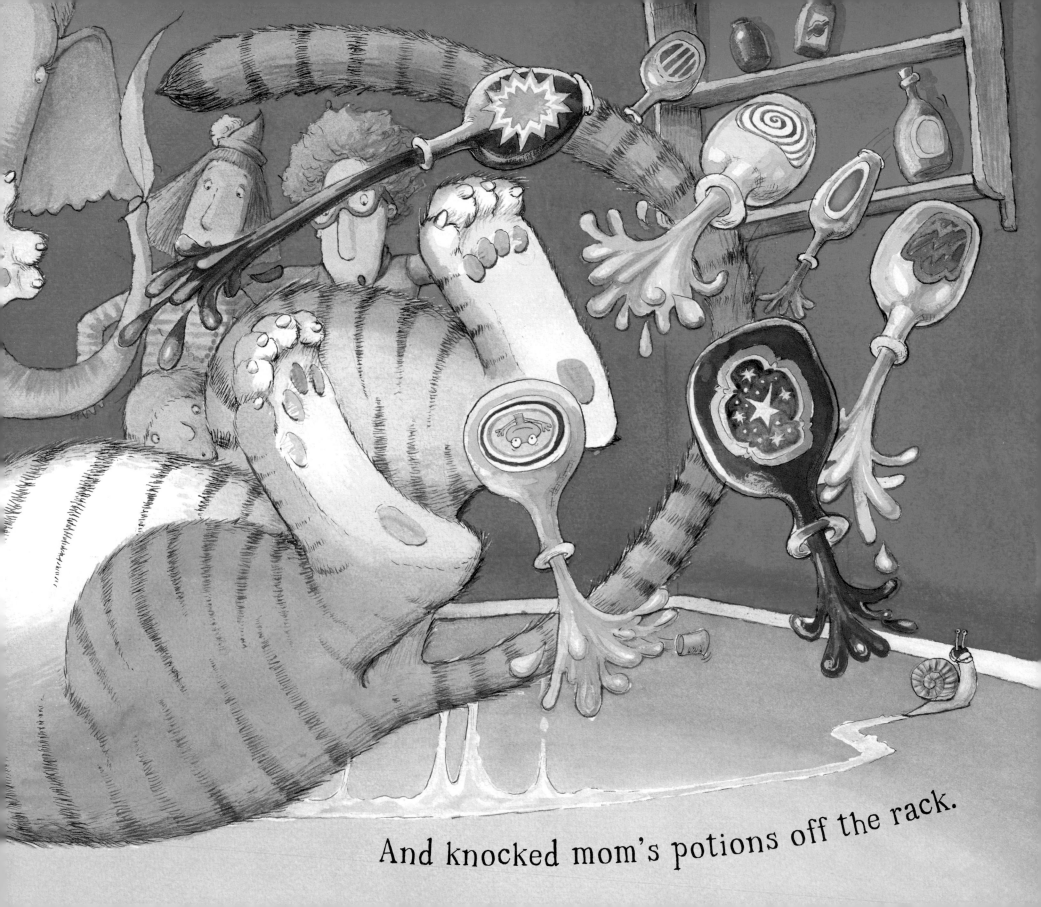

And knocked mom's potions off the rack.

And suddenly a puff of smoke
Made everybody cough and choke.

But as the smoke began to clear,
Those crazy beasts had disappeared.

Well Mom and Dad were pleased as punch
And made that snail a hero's lunch.

Mom gently patted
Nigel's shell
And said, "This snail
beats any spell
And now with magic
we are through.

We'll soon find something else to do.
You see at last we know it's true
A friendship can be magic too."